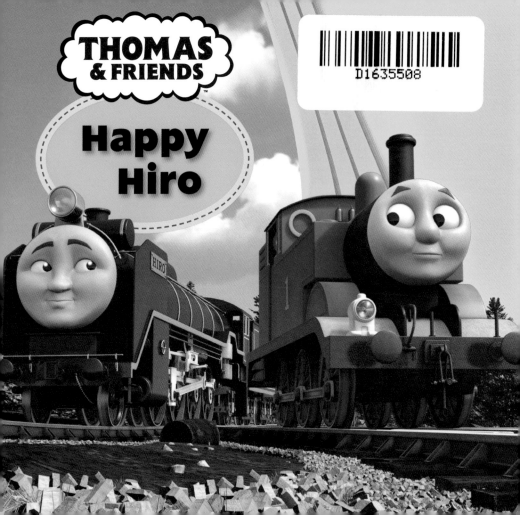

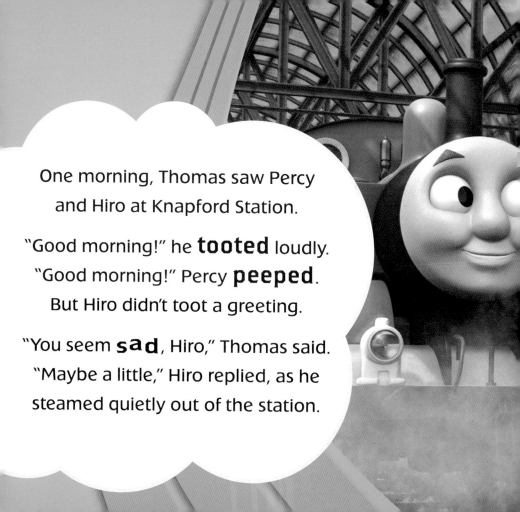

One morning, Thomas saw Percy and Hiro at Knapford Station.

"Good morning!" he **tooted** loudly. "Good morning!" Percy **peeped**. But Hiro didn't toot a greeting.

"You seem **sad**, Hiro," Thomas said. "Maybe a little," Hiro replied, as he steamed quietly out of the station.

Thomas met Charlie at the Docks.

"Hiro's feeling **sad**," he told Charlie. "Can you cheer him up with a riddle?"

"Hiro!" Charlie called loudly. "What has four legs but never walks?"
"I don't know, Charlie," Hiro replied.

"A table!" laughed Charlie, but Hiro didn't smile as he slowly puffed away.

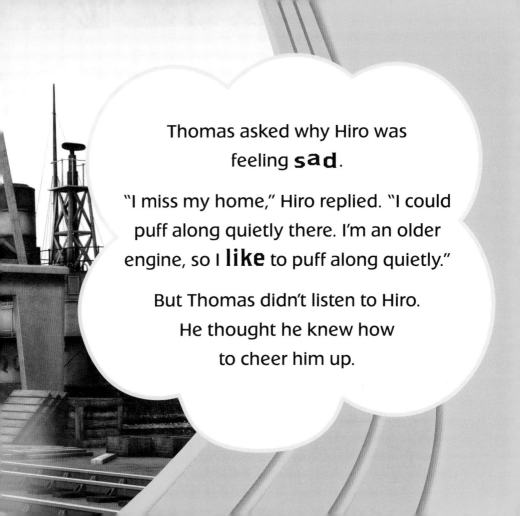

Thomas asked why Hiro was feeling **sad**.

"I miss my home," Hiro replied. "I could puff along quietly there. I'm an older engine, so I **like** to puff along quietly."

But Thomas didn't listen to Hiro. He thought he knew how to cheer him up.

Thomas took Hiro to the Hollow Tree tunnel. Hiro **smiled** when he heard the birds singing.

But Thomas didn't listen to the birds. "This will make you happy!" he said, as he **raced** along the tunnel.

Hiro was tired. "I just want to puff along quietly," he said.
But Thomas had another idea.

Thomas took Hiro to Misty Island.

Hiro **smiled** when he saw the sea, but Thomas didn't look at it. "Come on!" Thomas said, as he **raced** along the bumpy tracks.

"I just want to puff along quietly," Hiro said.
But Thomas didn't listen.

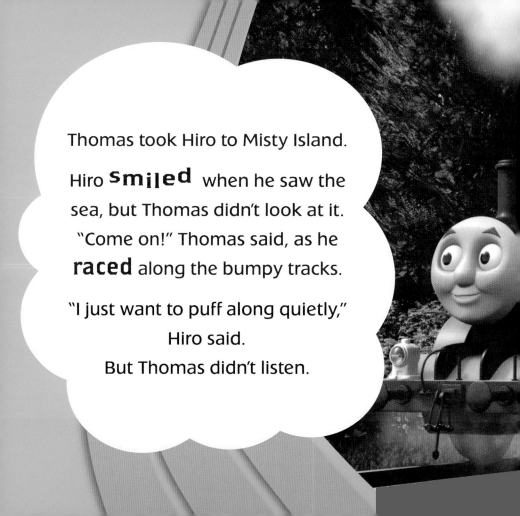

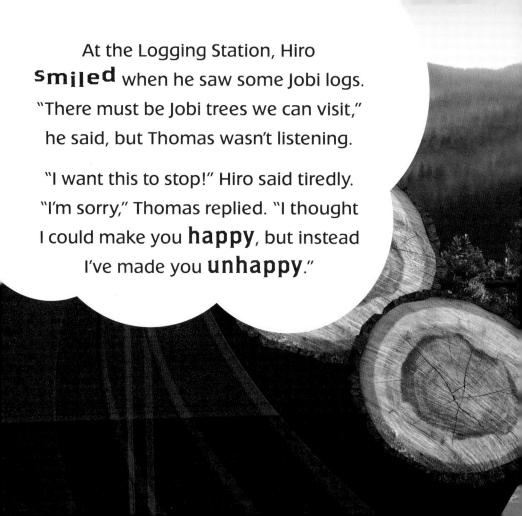

At the Logging Station, Hiro **smiled** when he saw some Jobi logs. "There must be Jobi trees we can visit," he said, but Thomas wasn't listening.

"I want this to stop!" Hiro said tiredly. "I'm sorry," Thomas replied. "I thought I could make you **happy**, but instead I've made you **unhappy**."

Thomas tooted softly as he realised where he had gone wrong.

"Hiro! You told me what makes you happy, but I didn't listen. Would you puff along **quietly** with me now?" he asked gently.

"Of course, Thomas," Hiro smiled. "I would be **happy** to."

First Thomas took Hiro
to look at the sea.

"This is **beautiful**," Hiro said.
"It's just like home."

"Can I take you somewhere
else to puff along quietly?"
Thomas asked.

"Of course, Thomas,"
Hiro **smiled**.

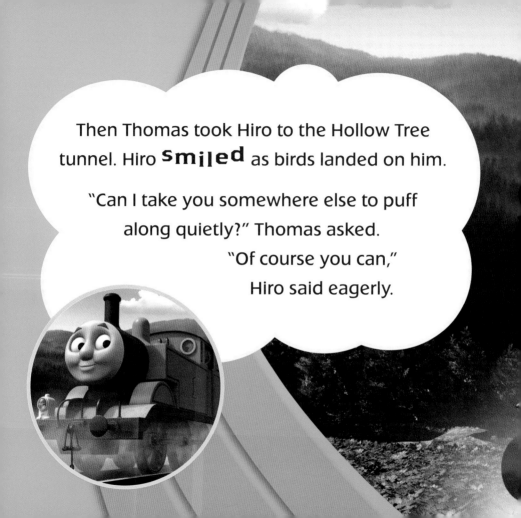

Then Thomas took Hiro to the Hollow Tree tunnel. Hiro **smiled** as birds landed on him.

"Can I take you somewhere else to puff along quietly?" Thomas asked.

"Of course you can," Hiro said eagerly.

Thomas took Hiro to see
where the Jobi trees grew.

Hiro gasped when he saw
the magnificent trees.

"This is **wonderful**. I am very
happy!" Hiro told Thomas,
and he smiled his **biggest
smile** of the day.

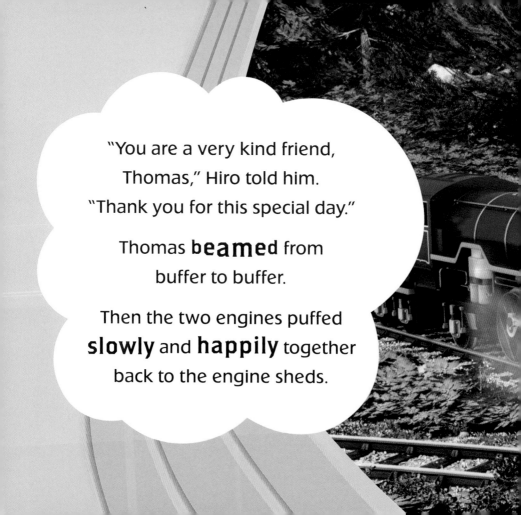

"You are a very kind friend, Thomas," Hiro told him. "Thank you for this special day."

Thomas **beamed** from buffer to buffer.

Then the two engines puffed **slowly** and **happily** together back to the engine sheds.

PEEP! PEEP!

The End